I CAN AND I WILL! I AM THE
GREATEST! I BELIEVE IN ME!
I AM BRAVE! I AM STRONG!

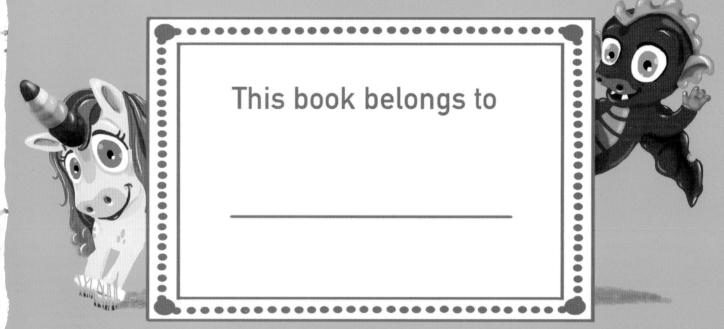

This book belongs to

_____

I HAVE MANY GIFTS AND
TALENTS! I AM SPECIAL
AND ONE-OF-A-KIND! I AM
HELPFUL! I DO MY BEST IN
WORK AND TASKS! I AM A
TEAM PLAYER! I AM LOVED!

To my little loves, Billy and Luke, may you always remember the magic words and take them with you wherever you go. Never forget that you are special, loved, and made perfectly just as you are! I **BELIEVE** in you and your dreams, and know you're capable of doing amazing things. Go out and share your talents with the world, because you were born to shine!

www.mascotbooks.com

Hailey Unicorn's Magic Words

For more information, please contact:
Mascot Books
620 Herndon Parkway, Suite 320
Herndon, VA 20170
info@mascotbooks.com

Library of Congress Control Number: 2020902742

CPSIA Code: PRT0320A
ISBN-13: 978-1-64543-431-3

Printed in the United States

HAILEY UNICORN'S
MAGIC WORDS

I AM SPECIAL AND ONE OF A KIND

Tracie Main
Illustrations by Justo Borrero

It all started the day baby Hailey was born. She knew she was different than the other horses, because of her unusual big horn.

At first, Hailey tried to conceal it and cover it with all sorts of things, and it worked. . . for a while.

But then, Hailey's horn kept growing and got bigger, and bigger, and eventually too big to hide.

Hailey whinnied to her mommy as tears shed, "I'm afraid nobody will like me when they find out I have this thing on my head. I'm much different than them—I'll never fit in!"

Hailey's mommy knew her daughter was quite extraordinary and perfectly made, so she assured her not to worry and told her to repeat these magic words after her: "I am special, one-of-a-kind, and born to shine!"

So, she did.

Down in the pastures, where the horses all roamed, Hailey tried her best to play and get along, but her horn always got in the way and weighed her down.

When they'd race, she'd start off in first place, but then tire and fall to last place. And during a game of hide-n-seek, her unruly mane would always give her away.

Eventually, all of this took a toll, and so she left the games and went to the watering hole. There, she felt safe and could let her horn go.

Meanwhile, across Meadow Land in another land called Swamp Land, there lived a dinosaur who felt alone and spent most of his time hiding behind a stone.

It all started the day Baby Blaze was born. He knew he was different than the rest, because he had large wings and big chomps accompanied by fiery breath.

At first, he put his differences aside, and found ways to play and get along. But eventually his wings and chomps grew out of control, and soon all the others were afraid because he had no self-control.

To ensure others could be safe and out of harm's way, Blaze decided that it was best for him to leave Swamp Land, so he said goodbye and went on his way that same day.

On his journey he quickly realized he was much lonelier than before. There was no one to talk to, no one to play with, just him by himself, and now he was so far away.

As Blaze kept on, he passed through Meadow Land and took a rest at the watering hole. Then, something caught his eyes. The most beautiful rainbow in the sky. *Perhaps this is a dream?* he thought. *A figment of my imagination?*

Then, Blaze realized it wasn't in the sky, but rather right by his side.

"Unicorn, with the most brilliant rainbow light, what makes me so lucky to be in your sight?"

A startled Hailey quickly hid her horn and said, "No, you must be mistaken."

Blaze exclaimed, "I saw with my own eyes a majestic light, so beautiful and bright. Please don't keep it from my sight."

Hailey remembered her mommy's magic words and declared, "I am special, one-of-a-kind, and born to shine!" And with that, she brushed her mane out of the way and uncovered her horn.

Blaze was so amazed and said, "Let's be friends. I'm Blaze, what's your name?"

"I'm Hailey, nice to meet you. What brings a Dragon to Meadow Land?"

"Dragon?! I'm a dinosaur!" Blaze couldn't contain himself, and roared a deep fiery chuckle. He rolled side to side with outstretched wings and charred the leaves off all the trees.

Hailey stood back, laughed and said, "Yes, what brings a Dragon to Meadow Land?"

"Well, if you can imagine, I became too dangerous for my friends," explained Blaze.

"Not too dangerous for me. All I see is a gentle creature full of passion. Now, let's see what else you can do, but first you must repeat these magic words after me: 'I am special, one-of-kind, and born to shine!'"

So, he did.

And wouldn't you know, the two of them had so much fun and played all day long. Blaze performed cool fiery tricks and Hailey let her rainbow shine the whole time.

As the sun started to set, Blaze began to miss his home and told Hailey, "So long, let's play again real soon."

And, for the first time, Blaze raised his wings and flew.

It was then and there that Hailey also knew what she must do, and decided it was time to finally let her true colors be shown. So, she headed to the pastures and let it be known.

The horses all stopped what they were doing and stared. Then, one by one, the horses gathered around, pointed to her horn, and said, "How did you get that crown? We want one for our own."

Hailey knew she was special and one-of-a-kind,
and she replied, with a smile, "I'm a Unicorn,
and I was born to shine."

And all the horses bowed down.

ABOUT THE AUTHOR

Tracie Main attended the University of Iowa as a theatre arts major, then moved to Los Angeles where she landed several roles in television and became an active member of the SAG Union. Tracie has always been a writer at heart and has written many published and unpublished works. Her keen understanding of character development as an actress contributed to the successful creation of her children's books. She was taught at a young age by her father, beauty industry leader and educator John Amico, about the power of self-belief. Her passion is teaching children to believe in themselves and that they're capable of accomplishing great things. She currently resides in Chicago with her husband and two young boys. Tracie is available to conduct workshops for your school, library, or event.

Visit **www.traciemain.com** to book an author visit or workshop.

ALSO AVAILABLE

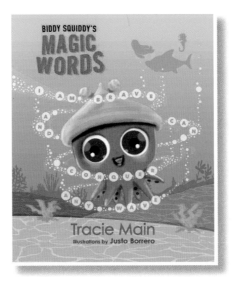

BIDDY SQUIDDY'S MAGIC WORDS

"I am brave and can conquer any wave!"

Helping build courage & self-belief in kids!